HORRORS OF THE NIGHT

Part 1

A Collection of Short Stories

TOM COLEMAN

HORRORS OF THE NIGHT

Part 1

TOM COLEMAN

Copyright

This is a work of fiction. Names, characters, places, and incidents either are products of the author's imagination or are used fictitiously. Any similarity to actual events or locales or persons, living or dead, is entirely coincidental.

Horrors of the Night 1
BN Publishing
ISBN 978-5-5700-9391-1

ABOUT THE AUTHOR

"This book is horror redefined. Dark and with more twists than a labyrinth. I look forward to reading more from this author." Amazon reader about Horrors Next Door collection

Since he was a child, he shared a great interest in riddles, mystery and the abnormal. He loved the thrill of having his mind puzzled and astonished by an enigma.

Today, he writes books for people who share his enthusiasm for scary and mystifying stories. If you love horror mystery you will love his books.

We are gathering all people with a passion for Horror/Mystery/Thrillers in our special group. If you want to be in and connect with us, join our group :)

Join here:
https://www.facebook.com/groups/541739063097831/

TABLE OF CONTENTS

HORRORS OF THE NIGHT

8

TOM COLEMAN

BABYSITTER

9

TOM COLEMAN

HORRORS OF THE NIGHT

10

TOM COLEMAN

CHAPTER ONE

Rachel walked out of class annoyed. She couldn't believe Mrs. Gertrude had chosen today of all days to give them homework. She already hated math, and she hated assignments, but to combine them on the day she had to babysit was almost unfair.

She groaned while walking in the hallway, filled with other disgruntled, excited, or passive teenagers.

"Why do you look like you're constipated?" her snarky best friend, Sally, asked with a smirk.

"Why do you think?" Rachel knew Sally was just teasing. It was a good opportunity for Rachel to get some nice cash as a babysitter, but the timing was absolutely wrong.

"Just do your homework after school so you can have time to babysit at night." Sally raised a reasonable point, but Rachel still looked at her friend like she was crazy.

"Who does their homework during the day? Besides, you and I both know how loaded the Graysons are. Babysitting tonight alone will get me more than I ever would on a per-day basis when I worked at Burger King."

"They are also super creepy—at least, that's what I hear."

"Not them—they're fine as far as I can tell—it's the kids who creep me out."

Sally laughed at her remark.

Rachel frowned. What was so funny about that statement?

"You know how weird it is for you to admit that ten- and eight-year-old kids are creepy and still want to babysit them?"

"How bad could it be? They're probably just entitled as all rich kids are. Also, they seem secluded, and they don't have many friends. It could be good for them to have me around."

Rachel's friend gave her a knowing look, causing her to break. "All right, fine." Rachel raised her hands. "I'm mainly doing this for the money, not because I give a damn about

TOM COLEMAN

two rich kids. That being said, why can't I do both?"

"Fair enough. Just do your homework if you don't want to be given a zero tomorrow."

Rachel had a brilliant idea, but Sally beat her to it. "No," she said, "I'm not doing it for you."

Rachel frowned.

***

Later that night, she was finally ready to go. The young teen put on her best formal-yet-casual attire and headed downstairs. "Mom, Dad, I'm off."

"Make a good impression, sweetie," her mother, who was seated on the couch with her dad watching the news, said to her.

"Be on your best behavior," Dad added.

"Of course. When am I never on my best behavior?"

13

TOM COLEMAN

Both of her parents scoffed.

Rachel rolled her eyes.

***

Rachel didn't have to walk far to reach the Grayson mansion since she lived just a block away from the place. It was the largest building in town, and that was counting the school, hospital, and supermarket.

She reached the gate and saw the guard there. He was a fierce-looking man. "Hello, I…" she began, but before she could say any more, the man opened the gate. She looked at him awkwardly prior to rushing toward the mansion. Rachel liked the number of lights in the garden and the landscaping of the compound. There were a lot of red flowers, especially roses, and the lights were dim but varied. The distance from the gate to the main house felt almost as long as going from her house to the Graysons'.

TOM COLEMAN

Nobody knew much about the Graysons. They moved to town four years ago and seemed very rich, but they also seemed ominous. The patriarch of the household, Calvin Grayson, was a handsome and charismatic man who was very good with people but always found a way to not reveal too much about himself—at least, that's what Rachel's dad always said. Caroline Grayson, his wife, was a regal woman who oozed exquisite taste and poise. She was always kind to Rachel, and her family, as far as the teen knew, and Rachel's mom liked her a lot. Her parents did, however, agree that she never talked about her personal life or the family's life before coming to Verdon.

The most peculiar thing about that family was, without a doubt, the kids, Jeremy and Maya. Jeremy was ten years old, and Maya was eight. Jeremy was the more forward of the two, and his diction was particularly impressive. You could tell he had gone to the best schools before moving to Verdon, but they insisted he'd been home-schooled. Maya was very reserved, but her ball-like eyes were pretty creepy if you asked Rachel.

She reached the door, frowning after the long walk. If she shouted for the gateman, would he even be able to hear?

Rachel knocked on the door, and it opened.

Young Jeremy stood opposite her, a smile on his face. "We've been waiting, Miss Rachel." There was something off-putting about his smile, but Rachel decided not to read too much into it. "Please, come on in."

"Hello, Jeremy," she greeted while walking into the large ante-room that looked more like a hallway, and she checked out that area of the house in awe. "Holy…" Rachel said, stopping herself from cursing in front of the kid.

Mr. and Mrs. Grayson came into the hallway with Maya, who hid behind them. Gosh, she looked scary.

"Ah, Rachel, you're here," Mr. Grayson said with excitement. "Thank you for coming. We'll just need you to watch over the kids until we return. Should be like an hour or two."

TOM COLEMAN

Mrs. Grayson whispered into Maya's ear. The girl seemed angry for some reason, and Rachel made a mental note to ask her about it later on.

"Did you hear me?" Mr. Grayson inquired.

"Oh, yes. Yes, sir," Rachel said, a bit flustered. The house was so bright and sparkly, with many glassy pieces of furniture like the huge chandelier at the center of the hall, a glass vase, sculptures, and other stuff.

"I know it's a bit much," the father said, referring to the conspicuous design, "but you'll get used to it."

"Please, take care of my children," Mrs. Grayson said to Rachel.

Rachel wondered why the woman was so tense, despite the fact that she was about to leave for a few hours.

"They are… special children who need special care. Just do everything they ask as long as it is within reason, and try to indulge their… eccentricities."

17

TOM COLEMAN

She nodded awkwardly at the woman who smiled.

"All right. We'll be going."

"Better be back soon, Father," Jeremy said with an odd smile, causing his dad to frown. Mr. Grayson opened the door for his wife to pass through.

"Don't do anything stupid," the father admonished

Though she thought it harsh, Rachel wasn't about to say anything. It was her chance to earn some good cash, and she would like for them to call her again.

"Sure, Father. When do I not follow your orders?"

Rachel sensed some tension between the father and son, and she had to remind herself that it wasn't her business. "Have a nice journey, Mr. and Mrs. Grayson," she said. They all waved before Rachel closed the door.

She turned to face the kids. They were a stark contrast to each other. Jeremy kept his chin up, and he had an upright posture. He

TOM COLEMAN

looked confident… a bit too confident. There was something uneasy about the way he looked at her, as if there was something he knew that she did not.

Maya, however, was very reserved. Her shoulders were slouched, and she stared at the floor most times. Whenever she did look up at Rachel, Maya's eyes never blinked. Rachel knew it was not a good way to describe a kid, but she looked sinister.

"Okay, kids—let's do something fun while your parents are away." Rachel had planned to have some fun while making the kids believe they were having some fun, too. "Why don't you two show me around? I'd like to know more about you and this wonderful house, but it's too large…"

"Leave it to me," Jeremy offered. He grabbed her by the hand and dragged her along with him.

"W-wait—what about your sister?" she inquired, but Maya just glared at her as Jeremy pulled her away.

19

TOM COLEMAN

"She'll be fine. Trust me. Maya needs space to carry out her… experiments."

"Experiments?"

"Enough about her. Let me show you my room. After that, we'll check the green room where all the plants are grown. Then, the art study." Jeremy sounded too old for his age.

Rachel didn't want to upset the kids, so she went along with it.

They went to his room first. It looked like the room of a kid who was far too wise for his age. She saw more books than she ever expected to see in a ten-year-old's room. "Wow, you read," she said, flipping through the pages of some of the books.

Wait—what? She found some very… disturbing drawings on some of the pages. What were they—torture devices?

"The Middle Ages," Jeremy said from behind Rachel, startling her.

She whipped her head around to see him staring at her with a menacing glare and smile.

TOM COLEMAN

He turned his gaze to the book and ran his fingers over the pages. "They had the best torture devices back in those times. So many innovative weapons that struck fear into whoever witnessed it, let alone those who endured the torture."

Rachel focused on the kid's facial expressions as he talked. He seemed fascinated by the macabre devices.

"We should… get back to Maya," Rachel said, trying to ease whatever tension the boy's reaction had brought to the conversation. He looked almost hungry as he spoke about.

"If you say so," Jeremy remarked, "but we haven't finished our tour yet."

"But—"

"I *said* we haven't finished yet." Jeremy said this with a tone of finality, and he took her hand and led her out of the room and through the large, confusing hallways around the house to meet Maya in the green room, where she was playing with some animals.

21

TOM COLEMAN

Rachel was shocked to see the blood—was she experimenting with living animals?

"That's … interesting," Rachel said, trying to take an enthusiastic approach.

"Maya is interested in some darker things. My parents get worried, but I feel she should be allowed to explore."

"Huh—is that so?" Rachel was on the side of the parent this time. They were right to be worried about that kind of behavior, but whatever—she wasn't her kid. All Rachel needed was to collect the money and keep quiet.

"Will you keep this secret between us?" Jeremy asked with his typical weird but confident smile.

"Y-yeah." Rachel was a bit confused as to what, exactly, was happening.

When she was done, Maya washed up, and they had some fun playing board games like Monopoly and checkers. Maya seemed stressed and scared. She stayed close to Jeremy. They were siblings, after all, so that wasn't too surprising in and of itself.

***

Rachel's eyes fluttered open. The lights were off, but one of the lamps had been lit.

What had happened? She remembered they'd been playing board games, and that was the last of it. Rachel looked around. She could tell that she was in the sitting room, and she'd been sleeping. Where were the kids?

She wondered if they'd gone to bed. Rachel rubbed her eyes. She looked around, but the kids were nowhere in sight. "Shit! The Graysons are gonna be mad at me if they come home to see me like this and this place as a mess."

Rachel scurried about, arranging the place. She went to turn on the lights, wondering why the lights were even off in the first place. She guessed they'd turned them off for her sake when she'd fallen. Such nice kids.

That was when she slipped on something and fell on her back.

Rachel stood up and felt around to see what she'd fallen on. The light on the lamp was not overly bright, but it was still clear enough to show her exactly what she'd fallen on and what was on her hand.

"Blood," Rachel said in shock. She staggered backward and slipped in the pool of blood yet again. This time, she fell on a solid body.

Rachel turned quickly around, startled, her body covered in blood. She stepped away from what she'd landed on. "Oh, my God. Oh, my God," she said. "Oh, my God!" She couldn't believe what she was seeing. She stood up and promptly turned on the lights.

"Mr. and Mrs. Grayson… Oh, God."

They were back… and they were dead.

TOM COLEMAN

CHAPTER TWO

Rachel rushed to cover their bodies while looking for her phone to call 911. The cops needed to be there as quickly as possible. A murder had been committed. Rachel couldn't find her phone, but a thought occurred to her: what if the cops suspect her? She was in the pool of blood in the middle of a crime scene. The maids were not around, as far as she could tell, and the kids—yes, the kids! Maybe they knew what had happened.

"This fucking house is a goddamn maze," Rachel lamented. Her next best option was to call the guardsman, but even he might suspect and accuse her. She recalled the way he'd glared at her when she'd seen him at the gate. Rachel needed to go with the kids if she were to meet him, and the kids were nowhere to be found.

"Gotta find them. I hope they are okay," Rachel said. She first went to the visitor's bathroom near the living room to wash herself

TOM COLEMAN

off. When she was done, Rachel started looking for them.

"Jeremy! Maya!" Rachel yelled. She tried to remember the route she had taken to Jeremy's room the last time. Why were all the goddamn lights turned off? The house gave her the creeps with the lights off. Add to that the dead bodies downstairs, and it was definitely not an ideal situation, nor was it what she had in mind when she'd gone there that night.

Where the hell was her phone, and where were those kids? How the hell had she gotten into that mess?

There was a sound, stopping her dead in her tracks. Every hallway had eight or so doors from what she could see. Was someone hiding behind of those doors? What the hell was going on?

"Is anyone there?" she asked, hearing nothing.

There were some sounds outside. They sounded like… raindrops? Was it raining? Rachel had to find the kids quickly, or she'd have a hard time explaining the situation to

TOM COLEMAN

anyone. Nevertheless, she had the feeling she was being watched, and that made her uneasy.

Her heart beat fast, and she was worried that whoever had murdered the Graysons was in the house and following her. Maybe she should stop shouting for Jeremy and Maya.

Rachel walked quickly without looking back, taking as many turns as she could before entering one of the rooms and locking the door behind her.

The room was… weird. There were paintings on the walls of some hideous and unnerving things: a person having their intestines pulled out by some weird creatures, a woman being set on fire… who had drawn these things?

Rachel decided to leave the room—she couldn't keep hiding there all by herself. The kids might be in danger, and the murderer might be after them. She had to be courageous. The money no longer mattered. Shit was serious now, and she had to protect the lives of those poor kids while escaping from the killer.

"Shit! Shit, shit, shit, shit!" Rachel lamented her cursed situation as she left the room and ran as fast as she could. She heard footsteps behind her, causing her to run even faster. Was she really about to die? As she ran, she tried to turn on one of the lights to see who was behind her, but there was no one. Was it all in her mind?

Rachel walked around the mansion for about five more minutes before she heard footsteps coming her way. Was it the murderer again? Had he or she found her?

She didn't have a weapon, so she balled her hands into fists. In hindsight, she surmised that she should have picked up a knife from the kitchen. Speaking of knives, where was the murder weapon that had caused Mr. and Mrs. Grayson to shed so much blood?

"There you are."

The voice caused her to yelp and jump in the air.

Jeremy was standing in front of her, wearing a cocky smile. "I heard you calling my name, but I couldn't find you."

"And you couldn't yell back to let me know where you were?"

"Mother and Father said we shouldn't yell in the house," he answered. That reminded Rachel that the boy's parents were dead, and he didn't seem to know.

"Jeremy, I need to ask you something." She knelt on one knee so as to be at his eye level.

Jeremy nodded and waited for the question with a curious expression.

"After I slept, did anyone else come into the house?"

"No."

"Have you seen your parents tonight night?"

"No, I haven't. They probably spent the night forgetting that they'd left us at home. It's typical, Miss Rachel. Don't worry about it."

"I need to tell you something, Jeremy." Rachel did not know how to explain it to the young boy, but he did seem older than he

TOM COLEMAN

looked, so coming clean was the best thing. "Your parents are dead."

"You're joking, right?" he asked with a smirk.

"I'm being one hundred percent serious." Rachel looked at him dead-on.

Slowly but surely, Jeremy's expression changed from relaxed to one of caution. He seemed deep thought, which was not the reaction Rachel had expected. Sure, the kid acted older than his age, but his parents were dead—why was he not freaking out? Had he already known about it? From his initial reaction, Rachel was sure Jeremy had been genuinely surprised at the news, but honestly, what did she know? She wasn't a lie detector, so she couldn't say for sure.

"Where is my sister?" Jeremy asked, looking very worried. It wasn't unexpected, given what he had just been told about his parents, but Rachel was more concerned with his reaction to his parents' demise.

TOM COLEMAN

"Why aren't you more surprised at your parents being dead?" she asked, curious as to how he remained so calm.

"All I care about is my sister, right now," the young boy replied. "So, do you know where she is, Miss Rachel?"

"I was looking for her, too. Where is she? I thought you two left after I fell asleep. You didn't hear when your parents got in?"

"This is a really big house, Miss Rachel. We don't see or hear a lot of things." The way he'd said it and the way this boy was acting… something was seriously off. For the time being, though, the best thing was to find Maya.

"We need to find Maya before the killer finds her. He or she might still be in the house, and I heard someone following me some minutes ago." A huge lightning strike outside reminded her it was still raining. In fact, it seemed to have gotten worse.

"Shit—we still need to call the police to report this."

TOM COLEMAN

"Language," Jeremy said, reminding her not to curse, but who the fuck cared about that just then? Rachel's main focus was to protect the kids and get out of the messy situation alive.

"Do you have a phone? Did you see my phone? I woke up and couldn't find it."

"Our parents don't give us phones. We are just kids, remember?"

It finally hit Rachel. "Wait! What about the landline?"

"Yeah, that's a good idea," Jeremy noted, "but first, I need to find my sister."

"Are you crazy? We need to call the goddamn police!"

"Not before I find my sister. What if the killer gets to her while we're heading for the phone?" Jeremy inquired. "I have to protect Maya, no matter what happens."

Rachel groaned in annoyance, and she placed her hands on her head. She could not fucking believe what was happening. Why was the kid so focused on his sister? Why was he

TOM COLEMAN

not freaked out when he'd heard his parents were dead?

A thought crept into her mind. She did not want to believe it, but still, all the signs were there.

What if Jeremy Grayson had killed his parents?

TOM COLEMAN

34

TOM COLEMAN

CHAPTER
THREE

Rachel did not know what to make of what was taking shape in her mind. She did not want to believe it, but everything going through her mind made sense so far. Jeremy had a weird affinity for killing and torture, which lined up with the brutal way his mother and father had been killed.

"Okay. We'll find your sister first." It seemed like the wise thing to do at the time. She had to try to find Maya to see what to make of the situation first. How did she even explain to the police—or anyone, for that matter—that a ten-year-old, mild-mannered boy had killed his parents? Even if they found the weird drawings in his room, would that be enough? Fuck, she should have paid more attention in civics class or read more about the law.

"Good. Let's check her room first," Jeremy said, and they both went. Rachel made sure to walk behind Jeremy as she watched him carefully. She found it hard to believe he could have done it, but it was possible. Rachel wondered if the Graysons had some sort of security cameras, but she did not consider it likely. A family that rich should have cameras, right? She hadn't noticed any cameras while walking around the compound, but then again, she hadn't been looking for cameras. She had been too in awe to notice anything like that. Nevertheless, wouldn't the kids know if there were cameras on the compound or in the house? They were eight and ten, so it was possible they hadn't been told. Rachel knew she was hoping for the extreme best, but it was an extreme situation.

"We're here," Jeremy said, opening the door to Maya's room.

Rachel entered. She noticed many pictures of animals, which wasn't that surprising, considering Maya's "experiments" in the green room.

Maya had covered herself with a blanket.

Jeremy went to meet her. Rachel was about to, but he signaled for her not to get too close. Was the little girl an angry sleeper or something?

"Maya," Jeremy said softly, "Miss Rachel is here. She just told me that Mom and Dad were killed."

Rachel was alarmed. Why had he just told her like that? She guessed that he knew his sister better than anyone, so maybe they had a different dynamic. Everything was abnormal about their situation.

Maya whispered something to her brother that Rachel did not get before she stood up. She rubbed her eyes, but Rachel couldn't tell if she was doing it because she was crying or because she had just woken up. What the hell was wrong with these children? One of them could be a killer, and the other was just weird.

"I'm so sorry, but your mom and dad are dead. Someone killed them, and the person might still be in this house," Rachel said to the girl. Her eyes looked so large and innocent, but they were still quite scary. Rachel had to look past that right now. The little girl had just lost two of the most important people in her life, and her brother could have done it.

"We have to leave this house and call the police as well." The moment Rachel said this, Maya looked scared. It was the first time Rachel had seen any real emotion coming from the young girl. Why had she not wanted the police there?

Maya's gaze turned to Jeremy, and he stepped quickly in.

"She's in shock. Can you let her rest, and then we can go downstairs?" It was evident that Jeremy had done something. Maya had known, and that was why she was scared of the police taking her and catching her brother.

"Let's go to the living room," Rachel said. "We aren't going to wait anymore. I'll go by myself if you two aren't coming." Rachel ruminated on whether Jeremy had taken her phone, as well. What had happened when she was asleep? A part of her was tempted to ask the kids if they knew of any cameras around the house—she didn't expect the surveillance

38

cameras to be obvious, nor did she expect them to be in their bedrooms.

"Do you know if—" Rachel began, but before she could finish, something hard hit her at the back of her head, and she fell to the ground. Rachel was disoriented, but she was still conscious. She turned around, clutching the back of her head with her hand.

"What the hell? What is this, Jeremy?" she inquired.

The boy looked more scared than she had ever seen him. He was holding what looked like a wooden rod. "I'm… I'm sorry. I-I can't let you call the police."

"Huh? So, it was really you who killed your parents?"

"What? No!" He looked so disgusted by the fact that she would even think that, which made Rachel question if he had really done it.

"Jeremy, don't do it," Maya said in a soft voice, tugging on his shirt.

Rachel was grateful the girl was there to keep him in check.

"Listen to your sister, Jeremy. You don't want to kill anyone else." Rachel's head ached. She was also bleeding, but her adrenaline had taken over for the time being. Rachel needed to get out of there alive. Fuck! If she had known the kid was crazy enough to kill his parents, she would have gone straight to the guard.

"I'll do it, as always," Maya said, and Rachel was stunned. Was she saying that she had killed their parents?

"It wasn't you?"

The boy's reaction said it all. "You don't understand," he reasoned. "Maya is a… special girl. She needs me to keep protecting her from others whenever she has her episodes."

"Episodes? How many times has this happened?" Rachel scurried away from them while still on the floor. She was scared as hell.

"We had to move after Mom and Dad paid off the police whenever she killed someone. It's only happened twice. I thought we all had an understanding, but then Mom and

TOM COLEMAN

Dad came back and told me they were taking Maya to a "special" home for special people. They felt guilty for what they had done for Maya in the past, and now they wanted to throw her away like a useless rag doll. Weren't they the ones who had brought her into the world this way? And they dare see her as defective? I already knew what that meant. I was not going to let them take her away." Jeremy handed the rod to his sister.

Rachel saw just how insane she had been. He might have an affinity for the macabre, but Rachel had been the one who had seen the pre-teen cutting up animals. She should have known better, but who the hell would ever suspect an eight-year-old of brutally murdering her parents?

"I confronted them about what they were doing. You were asleep then, when they returned, and in the midst of our argument, Maya took matters into her own hands."

Maya glared at Rachel as she came closer. That close to the murderer, Rachel could definitely tell the little girl was sick in the head and needed to be taken care of by any means

41

TOM COLEMAN

necessary. Right then, though, she had to stay alive and protect herself from certain death. If she died there, the kids could frame the story anyway they wanted. In fact, she was sure that had been the original plan.

"You killed your own parents."

"They wanted to separate me from my brother… my protector… the only one who allows me to do as I wish."

Do as she wishes? She called murdering people and animals doing as she wished? Seriously—what *had* she gotten herself into?

"I was not going to let that happen."

"So, why didn't you kill me after that? You wanted to frame me for the murder, huh?"

"We were still trying to work out the kinks of our story when you woke up, so we had to improvise. I followed you for a while as you stumbled your way through the house, not knowing anything. It's a convenient story: kids kill the babysitter who killed their parents."

Rachel, however, was not going to let that happen. She might be seriously injured, but she

TOM COLEMAN

was a teenager, and these were kids. There was no way she was going to jail because of this. There was a bigger reason she needed to end it there: the kids should not be allowed to live in normal society. They already seemed broken beyond repair. Had they been born that way?

Regardless, she did not care.

Maya swung, and Rachel lunged forward at the same moment, pushing the girl back. The siblings looked surprised that she still had that much strength and coherence left in her.

"You sick little bitch!" Rachel was filled with a primal instinct to survive and stop the manipulative children. The scariest and most unassuming killers in her mind were children, which was a nightmare brought to life.

Rachel punched the girl in the face with all her might, causing her to bleed. She felt a sharp pain in her waist and turned to see that Jeremy had stabbed her.

"You are not going to tear us apart," Jeremy yelled. "Maya needs me, and I need her. We are together forever."

Rachel grabbed his head and bashed it on the floor several times without stopping. "Then… you… should… be… together… in… hell!" She bashed his head after every word. He was dead before she'd finished speaking.

Maya screeched so loud, Rachel had to let go of Jeremy to hold her ears. She fell back.

"You killed him," the little sadistic girl screamed. She climbed on top of Rachel and tried to stab her with the knife Jeremy had used.

Rachel twisted the knife quickly away from Maya's hand and stabbed the girl. She stabbed her again, and one more time, just to be certain.

The little girl died with her sinister, owl-like glare fixed on Rachel.

The babysitter was injured. She knew she was about to die. Rachel slumped on the floor. She was ready to die. She knew no help was about to come.

Rachel glanced to her side. Her phone was under the table. Was that where they had hidden it?

TOM COLEMAN

She dialed 911, already knowing she would have a lot to explain.

"911. What's your emergency?"

"I'm at the Grayson Mansion in Verdon. Tell the county police to head over here immediately. There's been a series… ugh… a series of murders," she managed to say, enduring the pain before she cut the connection.

Just as her eyes were about to give way to the darkness, Rachel noticed what looked like a camera in the room. She smiled. It wasn't surprising that the parents, worried about their kid's uncanny behaviour, had placed cameras all around the house. She could rest easy now, knowing it had all been recorded… or had it?

(Based on the idea of my dear reader Constance)

TOM COLEMAN

HORRORS OF THE NIGHT

46

TOM COLEMAN

DARK SIDE

47

TOM COLEMAN

"Good morning, sweetie." Selene's eyes opened to see her graceful and loving husband, Damien. She was awake, but she kept her eyes closed, knowing he was watching her. He did this often, and she loved it.

"Hey, handsome," Selene said to Damien.

He smiled and gave her a passionate kiss. As their tongues canoodled, she reflected on how great it was to have the love of your life next to you.

Selene Foster and Damien Richards had been together for two years, and they were happy. She definitely saw a future with the man. Recently, though, things had been different. Sure, Damien was still basically the perfect boyfriend—he was loyal, caring, rich, good in bed, and smart. That being said, Selene could not shake the feeling that something was wrong. He had been distant for the past few months, regularly going to his private room to work there. After a year of dating, Selene had moved in with him. Damien had only one rule: never go to the

TOM COLEMAN

private room. She had respected that because he had time for her. Now, though, the time Damien spent with and on her had dwindled over the past couple of months, and it bothered her. Two days ago, he had spent twelve hours straight in the room. What the hell was he doing in there, she wondered.

"Hey, babe," Damien said. "I was thinking about inviting some of my friends over for a chill get-together."

"Oh, okay. When?" she inquired.

"Tomorrow. They'll be staying over for the next two or three days." That piqued Selene's interest. Why were they going to stay that long?

"What's this get-together really about?" She asked, giving him a suspicious look.

He simply laughed at her facial expression. "You're cute, hon," Damien said. He walked over to where she was standing by the bed. "It's just a get-together. You can ask Craig. It's nothing out of the ordinary. They're just a bit cramped at home, and I offered for Craig, Marcus, and Daniel to come and stay here for a few days so we can do guy stuff."

She squinted her eyes, analysing his face in search of falsehoods.

"Would you rather I go with them to a hotel for a few days until they feel better?" he asked, raising an eyebrow. "Think of it like this: you will be with us, and you can monitor us for as long as you'd like."

"You know I have work."

"Well, there's nothing I can do about that now, is there?" He made some solid points. Damien's friends meant a lot to him, so it wasn't unordinary for him to take care of them that way. They were also equally loyal to him, and they were all friends with her to some extent. Every girl has her insecurities, though. What if he brought girls to the house while she was away?

As if intuiting what she was thinking, Damien spoke: "You do realize that if I wanted to cheat on you, I could have done it any day, and I don't need my friends to do so." He gave her a knowing smile. Damien worked from home, and he was an artist, so he could manage his time as he liked, unlike Selene, who had a nine-to-five job in a corporate setting.

"Fine." She sighed.

Damien seemed surprised at her reticence. "Where is this… fear coming from?" he inquired. "Have I given you any reason not to trust me?"

She knew why. Selene had been getting more and more worried at Damien's secrecy. What the heck was in that bloody room? Damien was a man with whom she could see herself spending the rest of her life, but marriage comes with trust—could she fully trust him when he did not fully trust her?

"Come on—what is the problem?" Damien asked with worry in his eyes. "You can tell me. We are in this together. If you can't tell me, who else are you gonna tell?"

"What's in your private room?" There. She'd said it out loud. For twelve

TOM COLEMAN

months, Selene had never questioned his decision not to let her know what was in the room, but now, she'd gone and blurted it out.

"It's where I express my art," Damien said. "I am sorry, but I am not ready to let anyone see it yet. I hope you can understand. Hopefully, in the future, when I am more comfortable, I will show it to you."

"Is it that you don't trust me?"

"No, no, no, Not at all. It's me. I'm not ready," he tried to assure her. "You know what? I will show it to you by the end of this little get-together with my friends; how is that?" There was a piercing look in his black eyes as he smiled at her after delivering the proposal. There was something off about the way he'd proposed it, but she did not care. He was finally going to share the final part of his life with her. It was a great step toward their great future together.

"That would be great," she said with a smile. "To be honest, it has been bothering me for a while. I'm glad we're finally taking the next step."

TOM COLEMAN

"I am, too," he said, hugging her tightly before kissing her. She was so happy and so in love—why couldn't Selene let go of the pit in her stomach? What, exactly, was the problem?

The next day, Selene came home from work a bit early. She opened the door and went inside, and it was surprisingly quiet. Usually, Damien was playing some "Call of Duty," but instead, there was silence. She wanted to call his name and ask where he was, but she decided against it.

She made her way up the stairs, where she heard some weird noises from… the private room? Were those… screams? She was unsure. Selene had never seen the inside of the room, so she wouldn't know, but they sounded like screams. Was he watching a movie? The noise was not loud, but she could still hear it. What the hell is going on in there?

"What the hell?" she murmured, her curiosity piqued. For a second, Selene thought about just forcing the door open, using the fact that she'd heard screaming as an excuse.

"He isn't so stupid that he wouldn't know what I was doing," she said, presuming that the door was locked. Besides, he was going to show her what was in there in just a few days—why couldn't she wait?

"Damien?" Selene said.

The screaming immediately stopped.

"Are you there? I came home early from work. I thought you'd be playing your video games right about now."

"Hey, welcome!" he said from inside without opening the door. This made Selene cautious.

"What was that screaming I heard?"

"I'm watching an audition for a role. I'll tell you about it later. I was trying to get into the mindset of a woman in fear 'cos I was about to draw on that." That sounded normal, to be honest. She had heard of artists doing even weirder things to get "in the zone.

TOM COLEMAN

"Okay, hon. I'm going to get changed," but even as she disrobed, something felt off. Was there a woman in there? It was doubtful, but Selene had the tendency to be insecure, and this ate at her. Could she wait a few more days to know what went on in that damn room?

***

It was the day Craig, Marcus, and Daniel were scheduled to come over. Selene thought that Damien would be more excited, but he kept his attention focused on his phone.

"Why are you so fixated on your phone?" she asked with a frown.

Damien smiled. "I'm chatting on Facebook."

"So? Shouldn't you be more excited that they are coming?"

"I am. Who do you think I've been chatting with?"

"Oh, that makes sense. Anyway, I'll go prepare something for them to eat."

"Don't worry—I'll make it. I need you to go to the store for me, though, to get some extra snacks and stuff."

"Sure." He handed her his credit card, and she went to the store. It was a Saturday, so she didn't have to go to work. By the time Selene had returned, all of his friends were in the house.

"Seleeeene!" Craig, Damien's wild thirty-four-year-old lifelong friend said. He ran over and hugged her tightly. Out of all of Damien's friends, she was closest to him, and they got along pretty well. "I'm sorry that we are coming to disturb you two like this."

"Aww. C'mon—it's fine. You guys have known each other for, like, forever," she responded with a smile.

The rest of the day was filled with fun activities for the guys down in the basement while Selene did her own thing in the living room. A couple of hours after they'd arrived, around seven o'clock, Selene heard the sound

TOM COLEMAN

of someone coming from the basement. She turned around to see Damien looking stressed and tired. "You look like you've been lifting weights or something."

"I might as well have," he said with a weak smile. "Those guys have too much energy for me."

"I'll come down later to check up on you guys."

"No need. They're all fast asleep by now," he informed. "Apparently, Marcus had a big fight with his wife last night that lasted well into the early morning."

"I hoped they liked the meal you made for them, though."

He looked away from her.

Selene furrowed her brows in confusion.

"Yeah, they loved it," he answered, going up the stairs. "Anyway, I need to regain some energy now. I'm gonna have a shower, then go to the private room to draw a little."

TOM COLEMAN

"Okay." Selene knew something was off. He had been acting strange, and the mention of the private room always made her cautious, curious, and insecure.

After remaining seated for a few seconds, Selene made up her mind. She got up and tip-toed her way to their bedroom.

Damien had just gone into the shower, and she saw that his phone was still unlocked. Damien was a private man, and he'd never shared his password with her. This time, though, Selene was able to tap on the smartphone before it had gone off, allowing her to see his texts.

The first one that popped up read, "Make sure you do the sacrifice tonight."

Wait… what? was the first thought that ran through her mind. What sacrifice? Was it some kind of inside joke? She was thinking about asking him when her eyes trailed up to the top of the chat group. The headline of the group read, "The Cult of the Diabolus."

"What the hell is this?" Selene whispered, keeping in mind the fact that her boyfriend

TOM COLEMAN

was having a shower just a few meters from her. She read the remaining messages, and she was shocked. From what she could see, it was a legit call to kill people. The sacrifice was supposed to be the massacre of several people for "Diabolus," whatever that meant.

A part of Selene wanted to brush it off as nothing, but she continued to read, scrolling up to see the details of the plan. It was clear: the person chosen would get four people and sacrifice them in a gory, ritual massacre in an honorable offering to the deity they called Diabolus.

"Wait…" That was when it struck her. There were four of them in the house at the moment. Was it happening that day? What was in the private room? Who had been screaming before? She put the phone back exactly where she had found it, open to the Facebook group, left, and headed straight down to the basement.

Selene opened the door and went inside. The ominous feel of silence enveloping the basement as she walked down sent shivers down her spine. Why did

TOM COLEMAN

she feel that way? Probably due to her new revelations. A part of her still wanted to believe that it was all some big, sick misunderstanding, but Selene knew she would have to be a fool to ignore the signs.

She swallowed her saliva. Her breathing was uneven. She reached the bottom of the stairs and saw all of Damien's friends sleeping. Were they sleeping, or were they dead? The group said there had to be some kind of ritual, so that meant they could not already be dead, but it was all speculation to her.

Selene sighed, gathered her thoughts, and summoned her courage before going over to where Craig laid. His eyes were weirdly open, and he could move them, but his body was still.

"Craig?" She was confused—was he paralyzed?

"He's fine," the all-too-familiar voice she knew as that of her boyfriend said from behind her.

TOM COLEMAN

Terror ran through her body, and she struggled to calm herself. Selene knew that if she looked back at him terrified, she was done for.

Three paralyzed bodies and one lady who was a potential victim were all there in the same room as their assailant—it was a worst-case scenario.

***

As she always did when she was nervous wanted to remain calm, Selene took a deep breath and bottled all of her fear inside before turning to face him. "Hey, is he okay?" Selene asked. She had to be smart. If she had not asked why their eyes were like that, it would only make Damien more suspicious of her actions. "He looks a bit weird."

"They just drank a bit too much," Damien said with a smile. "Now that you are here, why don't we watch a movie? I'll get you some of the pasta I made."

61

TOM COLEMAN

"Okay, sure." Selene did not know how to get out of her situation. She did, however, know that she had to get him to leave, and this was the fastest way.

"All right. Cool. I'll be right back." He left. It was what she had wanted. Selene went to meet Craig. She took out her phone to call 911, but she wanted to be absolutely sure that a crime was actually being committed.

"Craig, I'm gonna need your help, okay?" Selene said to him. "Were you drugged by Damien or not? If you were, look to the left. If you weren't, look to the right."

The man looked quickly to the left. That was all she needed. Selene quickly dialled 911.

"Hello, 911. What's your emergency?"

"My boyfriend is trying to kill me and three others. Please, come quickly," she said as boldly as she could without being too loud.

TOM COLEMAN

"Where are you right now, ma'am?"

"Twenty-four Newport Avenue. Please come qui—" She noticed Craig raising his eyes as if trying to tell her something, but before she was done with her call, the phone was yanked out of her hand.

Selene yelped and turned around to be met with a backhand slap across her face. It sent her staggering backward and falling to the floor. She wasn't sure if the police had gotten her address or not, which was not good.

"Stupid bitch," Damien said. The vein in the middle of his forehead popped out, and he frowned at her viciously. Selene had never seen that side to him before. Was this the man with whom she'd been living all this time?

"You are trying to spoil my sacrifice. Do you know how long I have waited to do this?"

"Why are you doing this?"

"You know what? I am curious.

TOM COLEMAN

"How did you figure it out? Seriously." He seemed genuinely curious, and Selene felt it would be to her benefit to waste some time. Maybe the paralysis stuff would wear off, and they could all take him together, even though the guys would be much weaker, given their current state.

"Was that why you kept asking about the private room?"

That was when it struck her—the private room was a cult shrine or a place related to his cult. What the hell was in that room? Now, she really did not want to know.

"Ansa me, bitch!"

Selene was rattled by his shouting. "I just found out today when you went into the shower. Your phone was still on, so I peeked."

He chuckled as if impressed. "Not bad."

"Why are you in a cult? Why are you trying to kill your best friends and me, your girlfriend?"

"Because one must give up those whom they love the most to truly transcend into Diabolus's arms," Damien responded. The look on his face told Selene all she needed to know—he was a nut who had some strong beliefs. Sociopaths with convictions were the scariest kinds.

"You're crazy," she said. It seemed to hit a nerve with him.

"Crazy? For believing?" He pulled her hair and dragged her with him as he went up the stairs. "I'll show you freaking crazy! You wanna see the private room that badly? I'll show it to you."

Damien dragged her up the stairs to the private room, with Selene kicking and screaming every step of the way.

Once she was inside, it was a horror show. There were human skins and those of animals, as well. The room was colored red with some weird symbols drawn in black on all of the walls. There was a television and some weird, large pentagram drawn on the floor. Even the fluorescents were red. She

TOM COLEMAN

also noticed some ropes and assumed they were meant to tie up his victims.

"Please, you have to—" A crushing punch hit her in the nose, disorienting her, sending her to the floor, and knocking her nearly unconscious. Selene could only see and hear things in fragments after that, but by the time Damien had brought the three other individuals to the room, her mind was clear as day.

Selene had taken a penknife that was next to Craig when she was in the basement, and now she played dead, or in this case, unconscious.

Damien took each individual to a different side of the pentagram except for Selene. He didn't seem too worried about her because she was a woman, and she did not have a weapon.

Well, he was wrong about that.

"*Aktar luvre, nessus…*" Damien chanted in some language or devilish tongue she did not understand while moving toward her. He stopped to check his phone—

probably the Facebook group—and she saw her chance.

Selene sprung up and stabbed him in the torso, causing Damien to groan in pain. She pulled out the knife and attempted to stab him again, but he punched her in the neck. The poor lady coughed ferociously and clutched her neck as she moved backward.

The knife fell to the ground, and Damien was forced to go down on one knee. "Why can't you…ugh…why can't you understand?" he yelled at her. Was he seriously thinking of himself as the good one here? She could not believe it.

Marcus managed to jump on Damien from behind. The paralysis drug had worn off, but he was still weak. Marcus tried shoving his fingers deep into Damien's eye.

"Aaaarrrgh!" Damien screamed as he tried to stop his assailant from going any further. He felt his way to the knife, grabbed it, and stabbed Marcus in the eye.

"Oh, my God," Selene managed to say amid her coughs. He had just killed him!

TOM COLEMAN

Damien first dragged Marcus's lifeless body to his original spot on the pentagram. To Selene, it seemed like an important part of the ritual; otherwise, he would have just come after her.

"Stupid ungrateful assholes," he said, finally turning his attention to her.

"Forgive us for not thanking you for killing us," she retorted.

Just as he was about to come after her, the other two men each grabbed one of his legs. In that split second, Selene ran at him and pushed him to the floor. She shoved her fingers into his earlier injury, causing Damien to scream in agony.

Daniel held onto the hand holding the knife while Craig held his other hand.

Selene's throat was injured, and her nose was broken and bleeding, but none of that mattered as long as she would finish what Marcus was trying to do.

Damien would not let go of the knife, no matter what, and the rest of them were

TOM COLEMAN

weak, so she did the first thing that came to mind.

"Eat this," Selene said, looking into her lover's desperate eyes before shoving her thumbs right into them. Considering everything that had happened that day, perhaps calling him her ex-lover might be more apropos. She enjoyed his screams and wails as she bore her hands deep into his eye sockets. Blood squished out in spurts like water from a hose. Some of it splashed on her face, but she didn't care. Her fingers bore into his eyes, even after he stopped screaming, and she stared at the horrific face of the man she had loved for the past two years.

The police arrived a few minutes later to meet a gory and unimaginable scene. Everything was explained to them, and the rest of the details were taken from Damien's phone after it had been hacked.

At that moment, as she watched his dead body with her hands still in it, Selene wondered how things could have ended up that way. She knew how, of course, but

TOM COLEMAN

still… what the hell was wrong with the world? What other mysteries and diabolical happenings lurked in the dark crevices of society? What was the dark side?

(Inspired by a true story that happened in USA some years ago.)

THE CURSE OF HERNANDEZ

71

TOM COLEMAN

HORRORS NEXT DOOR

72

TOM COLEMAN

CHAPTER ONE: Welcome, Mr. and Mrs. Hernandez

TOM COLEMAN

Carlos and Christina Hernandez were happy. As they drove to their newly-purchased home, Christina squeezed her true love's hand.

Carlos smiled. This was the life he had dreamed of for years, ever since he was a kid. Now, at the age of thirty, the woman of his dreams by his side, Carlos was happy that he was going to see it manifest. He just wished *she* was there to see it.

"What's wrong, babe?" Christina said, noticing her man's changed facial expression.

"It's just… I wish *she* was here to share this moment with us."

Christina understood it was a sore spot for Carlos. "I understand, my love," Christina said, rubbing his hand. "I'm sure she is looking down on us from heaven with a smile. She is happy for us."

"Yeah, I hope so."

They drove for a little while before arriving at the home of their dreams, a four-

TOM COLEMAN

bedroom apartment in a secluded area of El Paso. Carlos still could not believe he had come so far, considering from where he'd started. He knew how hard he had fought his way from his lowly upbringing to reach where he was.

They got out of the car to look around. Carlos had never been one to care about neighbours, but the only reason he was initially sceptical about the place was the distance between houses. He was told that the area was undeveloped, and that was why it was cheaper. It would soon be overrun with neighbours, building their own houses, so he got a bargain.

Now, looking at the trees, bushes, and shrubs around him, the young man felt uneasy. There was something ominous about the place, but he couldn't quite put his finger on it. He was probably just being paranoid. More importantly, Christina loved the place.

He turned to see his wife smiling as she gazed around. She was happy, and if she was happy, so was he.

"This is great," she said. She walked over to him and kissed him. Christina didn't have the rough childhood Carlos had, but she had made many mistakes that still haunted her. Nevertheless, if someone like her could find love, anyone could. She had turned her life around after her teenage days and was now a newly-married twenty-six-year-old with a bright future ahead of her. Next would be kids, which was why they had bought the four-bedroom flat.

"Let's go inside our *home,*" he said, and she smiled.

Carlos felt something on the back of his neck as he walked away. It felt like a nail or something sharp had been pushed slowly into his flesh. He turned quickly but saw no one.

"What is it? Are you okay?"

"Yeah," he replied, though it sounded unconvincing, even to his own ears.

They went into the house. The lights were off. Carlos could have sworn he saw what looked like the silhouette of a large

TOM COLEMAN

man standing at the end of the entrance when they opened the door and the light from the outside had momentarily pierced the darkness of the house. He blinked; there was no such figure.

He turned on the lights, and the house looked beautiful, as expected.

"Looks like the moving company has already brought in some of the other stuff," Christina mused, noticing the couch they'd had in their previous place. "Let's look around."

"We already looked around when we were appraising the house, Christina," he said, but he followed her nonetheless. Christina was a bundle of energy, and that was one of the things he absolutely loved about her.

They went to all the areas on the ground floor: the kitchen, the dining area, the living room, the store, and the guest room.

"Let's go upstairs," Christina said, dragging him yet again to the stairs.

TOM COLEMAN

Carlos wondered how she still had that much energy after running around as they went up the stairs and walked down the dark hallway.

"Where was the switch again?" Carlos inquired. Neither of them could remember. There was a window at the end of the hallway, though and some light shining through it, enabling them to see where they were going. The hallway had four doors and an attic door on the ceiling. One door, the last one on the left, led to the master bedroom. Opposite it was the bathroom. The two doors closer to the stairs were the other bedrooms.

Christina opened one of the bedroom doors, and Carlos felt some intense vibes coming from the room. No new furniture had been added to or taken away from the bedrooms except for the master, but he saw a doll in the middle of the room after Christina had opened the door. It had buttons for eyes and a sewn-on smile.

"Well, that's creepy," Christina noted. She went to pick up the doll. Carlos was a

78

TOM COLEMAN

paranoid person—one had to be to survive the drugs and death-ridden childhood under which he had grown—but he was not superstitious. Still, that was one creepy-looking doll.

"Welcome," a whisper said from behind him. He turned back an instant later but saw nothing.

"My mind must be playing tricks on me today," Carlos muttered.

"Did you say something?"

"No, don't worry about it, darling." He did not want to scare her. As the man of the house, it was Carlos's responsibility to make his bride feel safe. If he was scared, she would be scared, too. He needed to suck up the growing pit in his stomach and be happy they had been able to get the house.

They went to the room opposite the one they'd just left. Carlos opened the door this time, and the moment he did, there was a sense of ease that came upon him. The room looked really nice. It just felt… fresh. "I like this room."

TOM COLEMAN

"Neat," Christina responded. She sounded happy that he was getting something out of the tour.

They checked the bathroom, too, before going to the bedroom. It was a nice, large space. All of their furniture had been positioned the way they'd wanted it, exactly as they'd instructed the moving company. Carlos heard footsteps. Not wanting to alert Christina, he walked back to the hallway, but he saw nothing. What the hell was going on?

Christina didn't seem worried about any of that. She removed her shoes and jumped onto the bed. Just seeing her happy alleviated any fear Carlos might have had. "Come on, honey," she beckoned to her husband. He went to meet her, and they kissed passionately.

"Why don't we really celebrate this occasion?" she purred. He knew precisely what she'd meant, and he kissed her some more. They had sex for the next two hours. Carlos was so happy. He felt so lucky to have Christina, and he knew she felt the same.

TOM COLEMAN

Later that night, Carlos decided to check the attic while his wife made dinner.

"Okay, honey. Be careful," she said, and he nodded. "Come to think of it, we never checked the attic when we scouted the house."

"Yeah, that's why I'm curious."

"Sure. Dinner will be ready soon, so don't take too long."

"All right, baby." He kissed her at the back of her head, a gesture she loved very much.

Carlos was tall enough to reach for the ceiling and open the attic. No sooner had he opened the trap door than a ladder came down, almost hitting him in the eye. Carlos was able to dodge it, but he fell to the floor.

"Is everything okay?" he heard his wife shout from downstairs.

"Yeah, just the ladder falling down," he called back.

"All right."

81

TOM COLEMAN

Carlos tried to play it down, but it had been close. Were ladders meant to abruptly drop from attics? He'd never had an attic in his house before, but still, it had been really surprising.

He climbed the ladder and poked his head in to see how the place looked. It was pitch-black, and a part of him wished he'd decided to check it out during the day. Wait—how could it be pitch black when the light from below should have pierced through and into the area? He looked down to see the bulb was still working. Why had none of the light emanating from the bulb reach the area? Was it him? Did he lack that much of an understanding of physics or space?

Carlos heard footsteps in the attic, and he looked swiftly around. Shouldn't there be a window in the attic? He couldn't see shit.

"Is anyone here?" He could not believe he'd even thought to ask that, but the situation felt weird, to say the least. Strange things had been happening in the house since

TOM COLEMAN

he and his wife had arrived, and it hadn't even been a full day yet.

Man up, he told himself. You've been through much worse. Stop acting like a little bitch. Carlos climbed up into the attic. He knew there had to be a window somewhere, so he tried feeling his way around.

He could hear some strange sounds, but they were faint. Probably his mind playing tricks on him again. Carlos felt the walls of the attic, looking to find the window. If he was right, the window was probably covered with paper or cloth. While feeling the walls, Carlos's hands felt some strange stuff. He could have sworn he touched something that felt like sand, but the moment he went back to the area, he felt nothing but wood. He also felt something sharp. He couldn't wait to light up the place so he could know what the hell was there.

Finally, Carlos found the window, covered in cloth. He tried pulling the cloth off only to discover that it had been nailed around the window to keep it covered. Why

TOM COLEMAN

the hell would the previous owners of the place go to such great lengths to cover the window?

After pulling and pulling, Carlos finally tore down the piece of cloth, but immediately after doing so, he saw what looked like a grotesque, ghoulish face with an open mouth reflected on the window's surface.

"What the hell?" He staggered back. His legs stumbled on something, and he fell to the ground. Carlos quickly got into a seated position and looked around. There was nothing on the window, but the light from the moon refracted through the glass and into the attic. With the influx of light, Carlos could better see the room and its contents.

It was… empty?

Wait.

What?

How the hell was this room empty? He could have sworn he'd felt some of the

TOM COLEMAN

contents when he'd searched the room. What was going on?"

It was then that Carlos noticed a suitcase in the middle of the room. "That's what tripped me?" He looked at the suitcase for a couple of seconds. Carlos tried to open it; it wasn't locked. Inside were things that looked business-like in nature. He couldn't see it clearly, so he decided to take the suitcase downstairs with him.

***

Christina hummed as she set the table, happy to be in her new dream home. She hadn't been too close with her family recently, but she was, nevertheless, happy to have a family of her own. She heard a giggle and turned around quickly, scrunching her face in bemusement when she saw that no one was behind her.

"Carlos, is that you?" she asked, but there was no reply.

She continued with what she'd been doing when the lights began to flicker. "And they told me everything was in tip-top

85

TOM COLEMAN

shape," she remarked, looking up at the flickering light bulb, disappointed. Christina decided to ignore it and keep on doing what she'd been doing… that is until she heard the same weird giggle again. It sounded like a little girl, but Christina knew that was impossible.

"Hey, babe!" she heard the familiar voice of her husband call to her when he entered the kitchen.

"I'm over here. In the dining room."

"Look what I found," he said, dropping the suitcase on the table.

"Did you hear anyone giggle?"she asked.

"What?" Carlos was confused.

"I could have sworn I heard a girl giggling."

Carlos's reaction changed immediately when she said that, causing her to be suspicious. His eyes widened and he clenched his jaw, a typical tell whenever he was hiding something. "What is it?"

TOM COLEMAN

“What is what?”

“You have that look you always do when you are hiding something.”

“I don't know what you are talking about,” Carlos deflected. “Let's talk about this.” He opened the suitcase to reveal some papers.

“What is this?” Christina asked, perusing them. “They look like bank records or something.”

"Yeah, and some other mundane stuff. It's written in a language I don't understand. I can't even recognize the letters,” Carlos added, also going through the papers.

“That's strange,” Christina said.

“What?”

“Our name is here.”

“Huh?”

"Yeah. Take a look." Christina gave the sheet of paper to her husband to see for himself.

TOM COLEMAN

Carlos was confused when he read their names in perfect English. "Why the hell would someone write every other thing in a weird language but choose our names to be in English?"

"Probably because there is no equivalent for Hernandez in the language," Christina said, sounding nonchalant. "Don't overthink it."

It was his job to overthink things like that, though. He'd grown up in an environment where paranoia was encouraged, and that was hard to stop all of a sudden.

"Just burn it or throw it away tomorrow, honey. Let's eat."

"Okay," he said, though he sounded unconvincing, even to his own hears. He put all the papers back into the suitcase and set it to the side.

They sat down once Christina had brought out the food and made cheers to their new home.

TOM COLEMAN

HORRORS NEXT DOOR

"Our first meal in our new home," Carlos said, raising his glass of Champagne.

"May it be the first of many," Christina responded with a smile prior to clanking glasses.

Carlos was happy to be with the woman he loved—why was he so diffident?

The next morning, Carlos woke up early to throw the suitcase away. He normally got up early because he had work. Christina was a writer, so she worked from home and didn't need to wake up as early. He did not want to wake her, so he decided to do it on his own. The real estate agent had informed him that the trash came once a week, and anything should be disposed of in the large trash compartment opposite his house.

The moment Carlos had left the house, he almost felt something pass through him—had it been an out-of-body experience?

89

TOM COLEMAN

He dropped the suitcase and started panting. "What the hell is happening to me?" he asked himself. Carlos quickly surmised that he needed to get rid of the suitcase and be done with the attic and all of the old things that had been left in the house.

"This is my house! This is my house! This is my house!" he thought as he stomped outside. When, at last, he had reached the trash and threw the suitcase inside, it didn't seem like enough, so he went back in, came out with a box of matches, and retrieved the jerry can of fuel from the car.

Carlos walked back to the trash, angry at the suitcase but unsure as to why. He sprayed the suitcase with the fuel then lit the match, letting it fall on the suitcase before walking away.

"Enough of this weird crap," Carlos Hernandez said with finality.

Little did he know that this would be the catalyst for the horrors to come.

TOM COLEMAN

CHAPTER TWO
Dissonance

Christina's eyes fluttered open. She knew that Carlos had most likely already gone to work; she had prepared him his lunch the night before, as she always did. She checked the time on her phone: it was 8:30 am. That meant it hadn't been long since Carlos had left. Now, it was time for her to get to work.

"I'll call him later," she mused, getting up from the bed and heading to the bathroom.

"Free," something whispered to her as she opened the bathroom door, sending shivers down her spine. Christina did not look back because she dreaded what she might find.

91

"Freeeee," the little girl's voice whispered into her ear again. This time, Christina whipped her head around to see no one.

"What is happening to me?" she wondered.

Walking into the bathroom, she gazed into the mirror, thinking about the voice she'd heard in her mind. What had it been? What had it meant? Who was that girl?

Her mind drifted to her past. Hearing the little girl's voice had taken her back to that fateful day when she'd made the worst mistake of her life.

Christina's reflection in the mirror smiled slightly. She frowned, perplexed at how that was even possible, considering she did not smile, even a little. Just to be sure, Christina touched her cheeks and lips to see if she was unknowingly smiling.

An even bigger issue arose when her reflection didn't move her hands.

TOM COLEMAN

"What? Wh-what is this?" She staggered away from the mirror.

"Murderer!" Mirror Christina shouted loudly at her.

Christina could do nothing but stare in terror. Her breathing sped up, and her eyes grew so wide, she wondered how they hadn't fallen out of their sockets. She was terrified… petrified. It might be that she was reading too much into things, but Christina knew what that meant.

She flashbacked once more to her memories of that day.

"Breathe in… breathe out…" she said to herself, closing her eyes and trying to imagine a version of herself that was calm and not having a panic attack. This was her regular routine whenever she had an attack. It was all in her mind, and she needed to let the guilt go.

After a few calming breaths, Christina was okay. She opened her eyes and was, once more, met by her own reflection.

TOM COLEMAN

She smiled. "You see?" she said herself, feeling relieved.

Christina opened the shower curtain, got into the shower, and turned on the water. "It's all in your head."

To her horror, instead of water falling onto her skin, blood did.

She screamed and fell backward, taking the shower curtains with her to the floor.

"Somebody, help me," Christina said, beckoning for aid, but she was too far from anybody's ears.

When she opened her eyes, there was nothing but water on her.

"What the… what is going on," she screamed at the walls.

Carlos was working at his job as the manager of the El Paso branch for the HomeGo shipping company, but he was unable to concentrate on his first day. He had

TOM COLEMAN

been given a tour of the building by Greg, the assistant manager, which was funny because the assistant manager of where he used to work had also been named Greg.

Now, after the orientation was over, he was sitting in his office, going through the books, but he could not make sense of the numbers because his mind was not really at work; it was at home.

"Something is not right," he said to himself, and he didn't mean just at home. The building, the one he was in right then—something about it felt strange yet familiar. It was almost as if he had been there before. Even the people working there all seemed familiar yet somehow different. Something was wrong with his head.

"I need to rest, man… or, at least, find a distraction." He picked up his phone, about to call his wife, when he heard a sound. The chatter outside his office continued as people packaged boxes, but the sound he hears was more musical, which was weird.

TOM COLEMAN

The sound hit again, and Carlos recognized it as the sound of a guitar string. Who playing the guitar? He looked around his office, but he was the only one there.

"We're free," a voice whispered to him. He tried to wave the voice away with his hand near his ear, and he got to his feet.

The string sound came again, this time louder than before. How could a sound for which he could not see the source be louder than the chatter and noise outside his office he *could* see? Nothing made any sense, but then again, nothing had made sense since he'd moved there.

He called his wife, and it rang a few times before she picked up the phone.

"H-hello?" Carlos immediately detected fear in her voice.

"Christina, what is wrong?"

"Nothing. Why w-why… why would you… think anything is wrong?"

"Tell me what is going on… now, Christina."

TOM COLEMAN

"I think… uhm… there is something wrong with me," she explained. "I don't want you to think I'm crazy, okay?"

"I won't. What is going on over there? I'm on my way." Carlos berated himself for leaving her there alone. Things were already weird—why would he leave her in that house alone? He was such an idiot for doing that, and he was going to make it right.

"No, you don't have to. It's just me having a panic attack. I'm seeing things and remembering some things, so… don't worry."

"No, honey, you are clearly not okay right now. I should be there for you."

"*No!* This is your first day on the job. We have to recoup the money we used to buy this house. If you get a reprimand or you're involved in some sort of issue on your first day, it will look bad on you. Seriously, just stay, and come home after work. I've got this. Let me fix my own mess." She seemed adamant that she was the one with the issues, but what if it was that bloody house? And what did she mean by remembering things? Christina was generally a cheerful person, even though she had panic attacks. She never did tell Carlos why they came. Was she finally ready to open up?

"We'll talk more when you get home, okay?"

"All right, sweetie. Take care of yourself."

She hummed in the affirmative.

"And if anything goes wrong… *anything* at all, call me. Call me… instantly."

"Sure. My knight in shining armour."

He smiled.

Carlos let out a heavy sigh after ending the call. He was worried… very worried, but she'd said she had it under control, so he'd just have to trust her. He had his own issues to worry about, besides. Something nefarious was going on in that place. Had it followed him from the house to

TOM COLEMAN

work? What is it, even? Why did he acknowledge its existence?

"Get it together, dude," he tried to cool himself. "Don't let them sense fear in you. You're the fucking manager." Yes, he was, and if he wanted to stay that way, he'd better stop letting his mind mess him up.

Christina staring at her laptop, the blank space waited to be filled with written words, and stared at her. She'd positioned her chair and table in such a way that her back was against the wall. This was because she was scared to turn her back on anything that might be there. She had been staring at the screen for at least ten minutes since Carlos had called. It seemed like a good idea to write something to clear her head, but now, when she actually tried to write, she came up empty.

"Fuck," she yelled, lifting her eyes to the ceiling. That was when she noticed something imprinted on the ceiling… or was it just her imagination? There was a symbol there, right? It was not absolutely clear that anything was there, and she wondered if this were another case of her mind playing tricks on her.

"Murderer," the same little girl's voice said right into her ear, only this time, the voice screamed, prompting Christina to cover her ears with her hands.

She finally started putting the pieces together. "The girl… the word murderer… my past…" It donned on her, and the figure of a little girl became as clear as day to Christina. It was a face she recognized and dreaded. The girl looked no more than eight. She had pigtails and wore a pink floral dress stained with red.

"You." Christina pushed her table away and got up, transfixed by the girl in front of her.

"Me," the young girl retorted with a giggle.

"I'm… I'm so sorry," Christina said, her eyes watering. "I… I didn't mean it."

TOM COLEMAN

"Why did you do it?" the girl asked, her eyes growing bigger.

"I—"

"You got away with it. You got off, scot-free," the girl's shouted, her eyes growing abnormally large. They were as big as a cartoon character's now, and Christina could hardly believe what she was seeing. She remained transfixed on the girl, paralyzed by fear and guilt.

"You think you deserve to be loved after all you have done?" A stream of blood fell from the girl's immensely large eyes.

"What the fuck?" Christina's heartbeat skyrocketed, and she started breathing heavily. "What… w-what do you want from me!"

"This is all a dream, so you have to come. Play with me." The young girl's face was back to normal as she walked over to Christina and took her hand. "Come with me. Let's play tag."

TOM COLEMAN

By then, Christina was completely lulled into her spell, and she smiled at her. "I'll do whatever you need to show you how sorry I am."

"Good. I wanna play tag. I'll run, and you'll try to catch me," the girl proposed.

What a precocious young girl, Christina thought. "Sure. Let's play, Susan."

"Oh, you remember my name?"

"Of course. I see your face in my dreams before I sleep sometimes. I couldn't forget you that easily, not after what I did."

"Okay, I'll run, then. You count to ten," Susan instructed. "Oh, and there will be obstacles to stop you from catching me."

"What obstacles? What do you mean?"

"My friends. You'll see." Her smile turned maniacal, her grin so wide that her lips reached her cheekbones. This terrified Christina, but she was hellbent on gaining the little girl's forgiveness.

TOM COLEMAN

"All right. Start counting." The little girl giggled as she ran away.

"Ten... nine... eight... seven..." Christina had not gone halfway when she heard a rumble. She was afraid, but she had already assumed it was all a dream. If she died, she'd just wake up. She dreamed about Susan a lot.

"Six... five... four..."

Footsteps approached the door, but Susan remained steadfast and kept counting.

"Three... two... one." She ran from the master's bedroom despite the footsteps. It was most likely Susan, anyway. This was her chance to catch her.

Christina was met by a large silhouette of a man with no distinct features. The figure was entirely black, with his eyes the only color.

She screamed and fell to the floor.

The man opened his black mouth, and black liquid poured out onto Christina. It felt like acid.

TOM COLEMAN

Christina let out something that sounded like a gurgle. "Susan," she called, "help!" She screamed from the excruciating pain. Her skin seemed to melt before her eyes. The pain as the liquid ate through her skin and made its way to her organs was too much for her to bear. And still, she screamed out loud, begging for help.

It was all over in a flash, and Christina found herself in the attic.

"How did I get here?" she asked. She saw Susan through the open window, sitting on the roof outside on what looked like a concrete slab. Christina thought it weird, considering the architecture of the house and others in this area, but she was more focused on the young girl.

"Do you remember what you did to me?" Susan asked, looking sad.

"Yes," Christina said with regret.

"Do you think you deserve mercy?"

"No," she responded. "What I did to you was horrible. I should never have gotten

TOM COLEMAN

away with it. I didn't mean to. It was an accident."

"And that is supposed to make it better?" Susan yelled, but it sounded more like a screech.

Christina had to cover her ears because the sound was too high-pitched. "I stopped talking to my parents because of that," Christina tried to explain. "I am a different person now, I promise."

"Did Susan have the chance to be different?"

"Why are you talking about yourself in the third person?" Christina asked, coming to her senses a bit.

"You remember the sight of my bleeding out? You *do* remember it, right? You remember what you did?" It was enough to cement the guilt back in Christina's mind. She was in tears. That had been the worst moment of her life, and now, she had to face her demons.

TOM COLEMAN

"You took the life of an innocent girl, and you got away with it. You are an evil person."

"I am… an evil person." Christina was near traumatized, hearing this from the very girl whose life she had taken.

"You don't deserve to be happy with your husband while Susan's family suffers in agony."

"I don't deserve to be happy with Carlos while Susan's family suffers." It was true. She did not deserve happiness after being such a horrible person. Susan let these dangerous thoughts fester in her mind.

Susan's figure Susan smiled. "Then, come," she said, holding her hands out to Christina. "We're playing tag, aren't we? You have to touch me."

"Will you forgive me if I catch you?" Christina hoped.

"Sure. You will be forgiven of all this and more. Just come outside."

TOM COLEMAN

HORRORS NEXT DOOR

Swayed by the false reality before her, Christina climbed through the window and placed her leg on the slab. The problem was that there had never been a concrete slab on the roof outside of the attic, and Christina Hernandez fell.

To be continued…

(This story is based on the idea of my dear reader Jennifer Williams)

TOM COLEMAN

Find out what happened to Hernandez
family and discover more scary stories in
"HORRORS OF THE NIGHT 2"

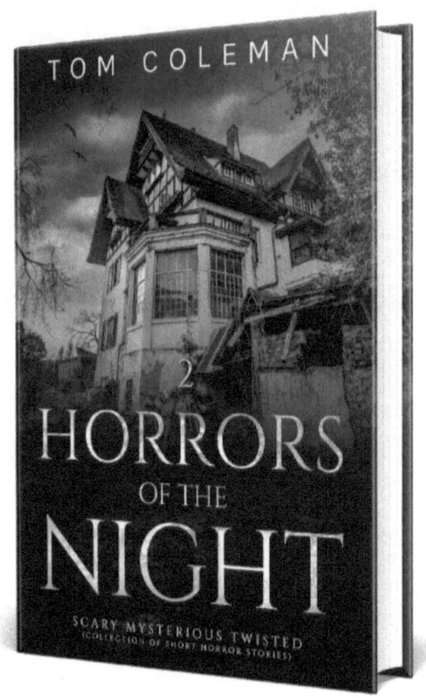

108

TOM COLEMAN

ABOUT THE AUTHOR

We are gathering all people with a passion for Horror and Thrillers in our special group. If you want to be in and connect with us, join our group :)

Join here:
https://www.facebook.com/groups/541739063097831/

110

TOM COLEMAN

HONEST REVIEW REQUEST

Dear reader, if you liked my book and want me to keep on writing, please go online and leave an honest review.

Your review means a lot to me, and it will encourage me to surprise you with more books and stories.

THANK YOU!

TOM COLEMAN